THE CUSTARD KID

TERRY DEARY

ILLUSTRATED BY
CHARLOTTE FIRMIN

A & C BLACK • LONDON

Black Cats

The Ramsbottom Rumble • Georgia Byng
Calamity Kate • Terry Deary
Ghost Town • Terry Deary
The Custard Kid • Terry Deary
The Treasure of Crazy Horse • Terry Deary
Dear Ms • Joan Poulson
It's a Tough Life • Jeremy Strong
Big Iggy • Kaye Umansky

First paperback edition 2001
First published in hardback 1978 by
A & C Black (Publishers) Ltd
37 Soho Square, London W1D 3QZ

ISBN 0-7136-5989-0

A CIP catalogue for this book is available from the
British Library.

Printed and bound in Spain by G. Z. Printek, Bilbao.

The Custard Kid Hits Town

A Cowboy limped into Deadwood Town. He was as thin as rain water and the soles of his boots were even thinner. He could feel every stone, every pebble and every grain of sand on the rough and ready road. His name struck terror into the heart of every spider in Deadwood; he was the Custard Kid.

The day was hot and getting hotter; the Custard Kid licked his parched lips as he decided to rest his aching feet and burning throat in the Copper Nugget Saloon. He stood at the swing doors of the saloon ready for a grand entrance, lifted his boot and kicked the door.

'Owwwww!' he cried as his tender foot struck the wickedly heavy door. For a moment he caught a glimpse of the surprised faces of the customers at the bar. 'Oooooh!' he groaned as the swing door swung back, hit him on the end of his thin, pointed nose and sent him sprawling backwards into the road.

'Who was that?' asked a cowboy at the bar.

'Oh, that was the Custard Kid; probably looking for some spiders,' answered the barman.

'Spiders?'

'Yes,' replied the Barman. 'He beats up spiders. Heh, heh, heh,' he laughed cruelly.

It was a cruel world, and the Custard Kid was finding out about it the hard way. He picked himself up, felt the swelling, red tip of his nose and hobbled off down the street with his travelling bag. It was a green travelling bag, with the initials 'C.K.' on the side.

A Hurricane in a Blue Checked Dress

The stage-coach waiting-room was cool and quiet; quiet, that is, apart from the snoring of old Josiah Hepgutt in one corner, and his wife Martha, in the opposite corner. The spiders spun their webs busily, knowing they were safe—this room hadn't seen a duster for many a long year. Josiah and Martha were not waiting for a stage-coach. They came to this waiting-room every day after lunch for an afternoon snooze, because they knew it was the most peaceful corner of Deadwood Town.

Suddenly a hurricane hit that most peaceful corner of Deadwood Town; the hurricane had red hair, a blue-and-white checked dress, a huge blue bonnet and an even larger grin. The door flew open with a crash. 'Hello, I'm Calamity Kate,' said the hurricane.

Josiah Hepgutt's eyes flew open and stared at the young lady in disbelief. 'I'm pleased to meet you ... I think,' he said politely.

'Me too,' said Martha Hepgutt, looking shyly over the top of her spectacles.

'And I'm certainly pleased to see you,' Kate replied. She took her green travelling bag, with the initials C.K. on the side, and placed it on the floor near the door. 'This town is so *quiet*,' she complained as she took a seat next to Martha. 'Are you folk waiting for the stage?'

'Well, actually . . .' began Martha, but Kate went on.

'I'm waiting for the stage to Hollywood; have you ever been to Hollywood?'

'Well actually . . .' began Josiah, but Kate was too excited to listen. She was bursting to tell someone about her trip to Hollywood. In the next ten minutes Josiah and Martha listened politely, while Kate told her story. She was going to Hollywood (the biggest film-making town in the world) to become a 'Movie Star'. A famous film-maker had heard her singing in the local saloon, and had offered to give Kate a screen-test. She had simply to pass the test and she would be a star. Kate's eyes became starry at the thought. Suddenly she jumped to her feet. 'Say, would you folk like to hear the song I'm going to sing at the test?'

'Well, actually . . .' Martha began, but Kate went on to sing her song.

'I can sing and I can dance,
I can act and play guitar.
If I'm given half a chance,
I will be a great big star.'

Kate's voice grated and warbled, bellowed and twittered as she danced around the room like a stampeded cart-horse. Even the spiders stopped their busy weaving to watch the performance. And they agreed that, while Calamity Kate might not have the best voice in the world, she almost certainly had the loudest.

'What do you think of that?' she asked.

'Well, ... er ...' Josiah didn't quite know what to think.

'You know folks, all that singing and dancing has made me a little thirsty,' Kate admitted. 'I'll just take a walk to the Copper Nugget for a glass of milk. See you later.'

Kate flung open the door to leave, and failed to notice that a certain cowboy was just about to enter. The door struck him firmly on the end of his thin, pointed nose, and, for the second time that day, the Custard Kid found himself sprawling in the dusty road, feeling the red tip of a very sore nose.

The hurricane blew out of the waiting-room the way she had blown in, leaving behind her a green travelling bag with the initials 'C.K.' on the side.

3

The Stunt-Man

The Custard Kid staggered into the stage-coach waiting-room and dropped his green travelling bag by the door.

'Hello. I'm the Custard Kid ... I think,' he announced. He was very dazed by the second blow on his nose.

'Pleased to meet you ... I think,' replied the Hepgutts politely. They were still dazed by the voice of Calamity Kate.

The spiders, on the other hand, were not dazed. When they heard the name Custard Kid they scurried to the darkest, deepest corners and hid, shivering. Word was passed around by cobweb telegraph that this was the man who went around beating up spiders, and in that dusty waiting-room twenty-seven spiders held their breath.

'That's a very unusual name, if you don't mind my saying so. How on earth did you get a name like the Mustard Kid?' asked Josiah Hepgutt.

'No, no. It's Custard Kid. You see, when I was young I used to be scared of things like spiders, so they called me Cowardy Custard.

One day I told everyone in town that I wasn't scared any more, and that if I met a spider I would beat it up. But everyone laughed at me. The name Custard just stuck to me and, even worse, I got a bad reputation for beating up spiders. Old ladies used to come up to me in the street and attack me with their umbrellas, and accuse me of cruelty to spiders!'

'You don't attack spiders then?' asked Martha.

'No,' replied Custard. 'Actually I quite like them.'

If you had listened very carefully, you might have heard a very faint 'Aaah' in that room, as twenty-seven spiders let out a sigh of relief.

'But I'm going to prove that I'm not a coward. I'm going to get rid of my Cowardy Custard label for good,' he declared proudly.

'How will you do that, young man?' asked Josiah.

'Well, I'm going to Hollywood, where all the films are made, and I'm going to do the most dangerous job of all. I'm going to be a stunt-man!'

'A what?' said Martha, looking puzzled.

'A stunt-man!' replied Custard. 'You know, the dangerous tricks you see in the films aren't performed by the actors, because the actors would be too scared. They're performed by

daring, brave, fearless, courageous and hand-
some men, like me.'

'Well!' said Martha, breathless with admiration.

Custard insisted on giving a demonstration.

He climbed on to a chair, and made Josiah pre-
tend to shoot him. Josiah fired and Custard fell
off the chair so realistically, that the old couple
were sure that he must have hurt himself. (Actually, Custard had bumped the tip of his nose on
his way down, but he put on a very brave face,
and pretended not to notice.)

'All that falling about has made me thirsty.
I think I'll pop over to the Buffalo Ben Saloon
for a quick lemonade while I wait for the stage-

coach. I suppose I'll see you good folk later on the stage?'

'Well actually ...' Josiah began.

'See you later then,' Custard called cheerfully over his shoulder, as he went to the door. He bent down and picked up a green travelling bag with the initials 'C.K.' on the side, and went out into the burning sun. He crossed the road to the Buffalo Ben Saloon, opened the swing doors very carefully and went to the bar to order a lemonade. But when he opened the green travelling bag to take out some money, he found instead that the bag was full of jewels.

4

Socks and Sandwiches

The Hepgutts settled down once more as peace returned to the waiting-room for a blissfully quiet minute. Then the door crashed open and a foghorn voice yelled. 'Hello, folks, I'm back.' Calamity Kate had returned.

'You know, I did a silly thing. I left my bag, full of all my jewels, right here in this waiting-room. Oh, here it is,' she said smiling, and picked up a green travelling bag with the initials 'C.K.' on the side. But as she opened the bag, the smile slid off her face like jelly off a damp plate. Slowly she reached into the bag and took out a pair of red and yellow striped socks, a packet of cheese sandwiches, a chocolate mouse and a book with the title 'How to be a Stunt-man in Ten Easy Lessons Without Breaking Too Many Bones.'

'These aren't my jewels,' said Kate pitifully. And that was true. Kate looked around in disbelief, then gave a yell which shook twenty-seven spiders out of twenty-seven webs. 'Hey! I've been robbed!' she cried, and with the speed and noise of a bullet from a Colt .45, she fainted onto the floor.

5

The Oldest Sheriff in the West

The Custard Kid sipped his lemonade and thought about his problem. When he had put down his travelling bag in the stage-coach waiting-room it had contained his book, his sandwiches, his chocolate mouse and his best socks. When he opened his bag in the Buffalo Ben Saloon it was full of jewels. He decided that there were only two possible explanations: either his fairy godmother had turned his socks into a string of pearls, or he had picked up the wrong bag. The Custard Kid couldn't remember a fairy godmother being so kind to him before, so he must have picked up the wrong bag.

He pretended to sip his lemonade while he looked over the rim of his glass at the people in the bar-room. Everyone was busy talking or drinking, and there at a table in the corner was the old Sheriff playing cards with some of his friends; no one noticed as the Custard Kid slipped quietly from his stool and sidled towards the door of the saloon. He had thought about his problem and he had decided that the only thing to do was to go back to the stage-coach waiting-room, find his own bag and replace the jewel bag which he had taken by mistake. As he reached the door it flew open and he was flattened against the wall as in rushed old Josiah Hepgutt.

For the third time in the space of half an hour the Custard Kid's face had been battered by a brutal door. His nose looked like a juicy red tomato, and he lay as limp as a pair of socks with no feet inside them.

Josiah Hepgutt screamed at the top of his squeaky voice, 'Sheriff, help, Sheriff! There's been a robbery. Sheriff, there's a jewel thief in town and a girl's fainted when she saw a chocolate mouse, and oh dear, oh dear.' He puffed and panted and patted his brow with a blue-and-white spotted handkerchief.

Sheriff Sam Simple rose slowly from the table where he'd been playing cards. He was a little annoyed because he had three aces in his hand and was all set to win a lot of money. 'Now then Josiah,' he grunted in his grating voice that sounded like a cow with a sore throat, 'Just steady on there, old timer.' (Which was a rather silly thing to say, because although Josiah Hepgutt *was* an old timer of 75 years, Sheriff Sam Simple was 76.) His white hair came down to his shoulders, and his droopy white moustache was so long that the ends had turned brown because they drooped into his coffee. 'What seems to be the trouble?' he asked.

Josiah Hepgutt explained that there was a young lady by the name of Calamity Kate over in the stage-coach waiting-room and she'd had her bag of jewels stolen.

'Stolen?' exclaimed Sheriff Sam Simple, his watery blue eyes opening wide in amazement.

'Stolen,' repeated Josiah.

'Oh my,' groaned the Sheriff. It was a long time since there had been a crime in Deadwood and he'd forgotten how to deal with criminals. 'Has the thief escaped?' he asked hopefully.

'Well, he's not there now,' answered Josiah.

'Oh good,' said the Sheriff, who didn't feel quite up to dealing with a rough, tough jewel thief. He straightened his shoulders and strode towards the door. 'Follow me Josiah,' rumbled the Sheriff.

'Where are we going?' asked Josiah.

'We're going to the scene of the crime,' he replied, trying to remember everything that a sheriff ought to do. 'I'm going to look for evidence, I'm going to question witnesses and I'm going to solve the crime. O.K.? Let's go.'

6

Barnaby Tupper's Dreams

Sitting on the hitching rail outside the Buffalo Ben Saloon was young Barnaby Tupper. Now Barnaby was just ten years old, and he was an orphan. He looked after the cowboys' horses while they were in town. They paid him 5 cents a time, and he made a poor, but honest, living. Every night at sunset he would go back to the old courthouse where he slept. No one ever bothered him in the courthouse, because no one ever used the place. It was so long since there had been a crime in Deadwood that the court-room had become as old and dusty as the Sheriff. It was a rather lonely life for a ten-year-old boy, but Barnaby didn't seem to mind.

Today was the one day of the week to which Barnaby really looked forward, for today was the day that the stage-coach came to Deadwood. He loved watching the well dressed gentlemen, their tall silk hats and the pretty ladies in their fine frilly clothes as they stepped down from the coach for a short stop in Deadwood. These were the film stars on their way to Hollywood to make the moving pictures which Barnaby had heard so much about, but never seen.

'One day I'm going to Hollywood,' Barnaby Tupper decided at the age of eight, and from that day onward he started to save every spare cent for the five dollar stage-coach fare.

He was day-dreaming about Hollywood when Sheriff Sam Simple came out of the Buffalo Ben Saloon on the trail of the jewel thief. Barnaby heard the Sheriff announce that he was going to solve a crime, and that sounded like an adventure not to be missed. He jumped down from the hitching rail and followed the Sheriff over the road to the stage-coach waiting-room.

'O Ye Fates ... How Could Ye Be So Cruel?'

Barnaby Tupper followed Sheriff Sam Simple and Josiah Hepgutt into the waiting-room, and there a heartbreaking sight met their eyes— Calamity Kate was sprawled across the floor while Martha Hepgutt raised Kate's head and was trying to revive her with a bottle of smelling salts.

The sharp scent of the smelling salts stung Kate's nose and brought tears to her eyes. The tears rolled down her cheeks and made her eye make-up run until she had two grey streaks running down her face. The sadness of such a beautiful young lady in such a pitiful condition was so great that a lump came into the throat of the Sheriff. At that moment the Sheriff swore to himself that he would find the man who had dared to hurt this sweet girl and he would bring him to justice. 'Can you tell us exactly what happened Miss?' the Sheriff asked as gently as his rumbling-thunder voice would allow.

Now Kate had watched this sort of scene acted out on stage many times, where the heroine of the play bravely pulls herself together and reveals the name of the criminal to the forces of the law. She had never been in the position of a tragic heroine before and she was determined to make the most of it. She answered the Sheriff in the true style of the great actress she thought she was. 'Alas, alack and woe is me. That such a thing should happen to someone such as I, someone who has tried to go through life without hurting a fly, someone who has had a smile and a song for everyone,' Kate went on, 'Someone who has walked along life's straight and crooked road and never barked up the wrong tree. Oh ye fates ... how could ye be so cruel?'

It was a beautiful performance and Martha Hepgutt would have applauded if she hadn't been using both hands to hold Kate's head up from the dusty floor. 'Yes, but what actually happened?' asked Sheriff Sam Simple, trying to get to the point.

'I've been robbed of course,' shouted Kate, forgetting her performance. 'I left my bag of jewels here for five minutes, and when I came back they'd gone.'

Now Barnaby Tupper had seen all the comings and goings from his hitching rail opposite. He had seen Kate go into the waiting-room with a green travelling bag, and he had seen her come out a few minutes later without it. On her way out Kate had nearly flattened a tall, thin cowboy who was carrying a similar bag, and that cowboy had gone into the waiting-room and also come out after a few minutes—but the cowboy had come out carrying a bag and had gone straight into the Buffalo Ben Saloon. Barnaby Tupper had never been to school, but he could put two and two together—he knew who the thief was, and more important, he could tell the Sheriff *where* the thief was. 'Excuse me, Sheriff, but I think I can . . .' began Barnaby.

'Just button your lip youngster,' growled the Sheriff, who turned to old Josiah and asked 'Now then Josiah, have you been here all the time?'

'Yes Sheriff,' replied Josiah, 'Martha and I saw it all.'

'Did you see Miss Calamity leave her jewels here?'

'Yes, Sheriff.'

'And did you see the thief, Josiah?'

'I certainly did Sheriff,' answered Josiah. 'It was a young cowboy; called himself the Mustard Kid. He's the thief!'

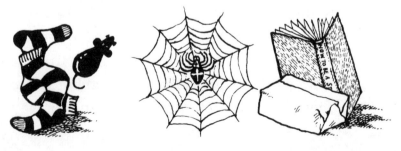

Barnaby's Buttoned Lip

Martha Hepgutt helped Calamity Kate onto a seat where Kate began to repair the damage that her tears had done to her make-up. 'Excuse me dear,' interrupted Martha, 'but I think you're mistaken. The young cowboy's name wasn't The Mustard Kid, it was the Custard Kid.' Sheriff Sam Simple's droopy eyes flew wide open.

'The Custard Kid, did you say? Oh, I've heard about him, a really nasty criminal. He goes around looking for spiders to beat up, so they say.' The Sheriff began to tremble at the thought as he reached into his shirt pocket for a piece of paper and a pencil. He usually used these to keep the score in his card game, but he felt that the right thing for a sheriff to do would be to take notes. 'I'm going to have to have a description of this Custard Kid so that I can send a posse out to get him.'

Barnaby leapt to his feet and piped up. 'I say Sheriff, I've got a cat if you would like to borrow him.'

'Button up your lip, youngster,' growled the Sheriff. 'I said I need a posse ... not a pussy!'

'Sorry Sheriff—I was only trying to help,' muttered Barnaby as he sat down again miserably.

'Can you describe him Josiah?' said the Sheriff turning to the old man.

'Well...er...he was young. Between twenty and forty years old, and he was thin,' said Josiah, screwing up his eyes tightly and trying to think hard.

Sheriff Sam Simple glared at him angrily and sighed. 'Do you realise how many thin cowboys aged between twenty and forty there are in the West?'

Josiah opened his eyes and smiled weakly at the Sheriff. 'Er, there must be dozens,' he suggested.

'There must be thousands,' corrected the Sheriff. 'Can't you do any better? Can't you describe what he was wearing or anything unusual about him?'

'Well, he had a very red nose ... and ... er ... I'm getting old Sheriff and my memory isn't too good these days,' pleaded Josiah rather pathetically.

Sheriff Sam Simple's moustache began to quiver, which was a sure sign that he was about to explode with rage. His card game had been ruined, there was a dangerous criminal loose in his town, and now there was no one able to tell him how to recognise the thief. Just as his blood reached boiling point Martha Hepgutt came to the rescue. 'I say, Mr Simple,' she said in her sweetest voice, 'Young Barnaby over there sits outside the Buffalo Ben Saloon every day. Now he must have seen the Custard Kid coming and going. He's as sharp as a new pin is Barnaby. Why don't you ask him Sheriff?'

The Sheriff turned slowly to Barnaby and looked at him sternly. Barnaby glared back at the Sheriff sulkily—he was burning to say 'I've been trying to tell you for the past ten minutes,' but the Sheriff looked a very angry man, so he stayed silent.

'Well, Barnaby, what can you tell me about this Custard Kid?' asked the Sheriff gruffly.

'He is six foot two inches tall,' began Barnaby smartly.

'Six foot two?' The Sheriff's mouth fell open as he pictured himself trying to arrest a vicious six foot two ruffian.

'But he's only about ten stone ... very skinny,' added Barnaby.

'Oh, good,' said the Sheriff letting out a sigh of relief. 'Any idea of how he was dressed?'

'He was wearing a black hat,' went on Barnaby.

'Wearing a black hat,' the Sheriff repeated as he made a note on his paper.

'A leather jacket and black trousers.'

'A leather jacket and black trousers,' mumbled the Sheriff.

'He had dusty brown boots and walked with a limp.'

'Dusty boots ... walked with limp,' the Sheriff's voice rumbled along.

'And he's standing right behind you now Sheriff,' gasped Barnaby.

'And he's standing right behind me now,' repeated the Sheriff making a careful note of it. Suddenly he realised what he had written. His mouth went dry with fear. His throat went dry with fear, and he croaked, 'And he's standing right behind me now?' Sheriff Sam Simple turned round slowly and came face to chin with a skinny six-foot-two cowboy in a black hat and leather jacket. It was the Custard Kid.

9

Kate's Calamity

There was a complete hush in the waiting-room for about two seconds, then everyone started shouting at once.

'That's the man Sheriff,' yelled Barnaby.

'Arrest him Mr Simple,' squawked Martha Hepgutt.

'Show him what you're made of Sam,' squeaked Old Josiah.

'Help, aaagh, help oooh,' screamed Calamity Kate kicking her legs frantically in excitement and deafening everyone with her foghorn voice. Then the shouting died down as suddenly as it had begun and everyone waited to see what the Sheriff would do.

'I hereby arrest you on the charge of jewel robbery,' mumbled the Sheriff uncertainly, his eyes half closed as he tried hard to remember the correct words for an arrest. 'I must warn you,' he went on as he reached for his handcuffs 'that anything you say may be taken down and used in evidence against you.' The Sheriff opened his eyes, quite pleased with his performance, and looked for the Custard Kid's hand to slip on the handcuffs. He found the Custard

Kid's hand was just a few inches away from his face, and in that hand there was a gun; and the gun was aimed right between his eyes.

'Sorry Sheriff,' said the Custard Kid politely, 'but I'm a little bit too busy to be arrested today. Just pass me those handcuffs, and back away to the far wall.' The Sheriff dumbly did as he was told and Custard quickly went into action with his desperate escape plan. He moved across the room and grabbed Calamity Kate by the arm. Kate was too amazed and frightened to put up a fight as Custard fastened one link of the hand-cuffs around her wrist, led her outside into the dusty street and fastened the other end of the handcuffs to the wooden hitching rail. He then went back to the door and waved his gun threat-eningly at the Sheriff. 'Well, Sheriff, the stage is due in about ten minutes and I'm going to get on it. Don't try to stop me, because if you do I'll fill that young lady out there full of lead.' (The Custard Kid had spent many years talking 'tough' and he sounded as if he really meant it, even though he didn't.) 'That young lady is what you might call a hostage,' he went on. 'If you let me get on the stage, and don't try to make trouble, then I'll let her go free. Understand?'

'Yes sir,' croaked the Sheriff.

Outside in the street Calamity Kate had found her voice again. 'Help, help, I've been kidnapped,' she screamed. 'He's going to kill me. Help me somebody, anybody, please!'

The Custard Kid grabbed the long ribbons from Kate's bonnet and stuffed them into her open mouth to silence her.

In one unbelievable minute since he had walked into the stage-coach waiting-room, the Custard Kid had been arrested, he had escaped, and he had become a kidnapper. And nobody in the whole of Deadwood was more surprised by this than the Custard Kid himself.

Barnaby's Plan

The main street of Deadwood was as quiet as a graveyard, which wasn't unusual, but today the curtains at every window twitched as everyone peeped out nervously to have a front row view of the first piece of excitement the town had known since the saloon dog had fought Barnaby Tupper's cat—and lost. A fly buzzed lazily round the Custard Kid and the sun beat down on his face. He leaned against the hitching rail and tilted his hat forward to shade his eyes. It had been an exciting and tense morning, but at last Custard could relax. He relaxed a little more, and before he knew it, he had relaxed into a deep sleep.

At the feet of the Custard Kid sat Calamity Kate, handcuffed to the hitching rail. She looked up at the man who had kidnapped her, and her face showed no fear, and no hatred—just admiration. All her life Kate had wanted to meet a real, tough cowboy, like the ones in the films, who would sweep her off her feet and carry her away to a life of adventure and excitement; and now it had happened to her, and the cowboy who had made her dreams come true was called the Custard Kid. The fact that he had grabbed her roughly, handcuffed her to a rail, gagged her with her own bonnet ribbons and threatened her with a gun didn't alter Kate's good opinion of Custard one little bit—indeed it made her admire him all the more. Kate looked up at him and murmured, 'What a man.' Unfortunately her mouth was full of ribbon, so the sound that came out was 'Uh, uh, mmm, mm.' Kate was content.

But in the waiting-room Martha Hepgutt was not content. 'Sheriff Sam Simple, I'm ashamed of you. How could you let that young thug get away with that? What are you going to do about it?' she demanded.

'Well, Martha, I admit I may have been a bit slow . . . .' he mumbled, looking at his boots.

'A bit slow,' she interrupted. 'A seventy-year-old snail could have done better.'

The Sheriff shuffled his feet uncomfortably. Barnaby felt sorry for the old man. 'I say Sheriff,' he said, 'I've got an idea.'

'Go ahead boy,' muttered the Sheriff miserably.

'Well, you still have your gun,' Barnaby pointed out, 'and he's standing just ten foot from the door. Open the door and shoot him. Even you can't miss at ten feet.'

'You're right,' said the Sheriff, brightening up as he saw the chance to make up for all his earlier mistakes and become a hero by rescuing Calamity Kate. He drew his gun and walked slowly towards the door. The door creaked as he opened it one inch, and then two inches. He saw the Custard Kid dozing against the hitching rail; he pushed the muzzle of the gun through the crack in the door and took aim at the back of Custard's head. Everyone in the room waited tensely.

Barnaby's Master Plan

But Sheriff Sam Simple did not pull the trigger. Instead he took his gun from the crack in the door and put it back in his holster. 'I've just remembered: I can't shoot him,' the Sheriff said.

'Why ever not?' asked Barnaby, Josiah and Martha together.

'Because I don't have any bullets in my gun,' explained Sheriff Simple simply.

'Ohhh no,' groaned the others.

'Well you see, I was cleaning my gun in my office one day, about ten years ago, and it went off by accident. Shot a hole clean through the left ear of the President of the United States.'

'You shot the President!' exclaimed Josiah in amazement.

'Well, not exactly. I shot his picture on the wall,' the Sheriff explained. 'Anyhow, from that day to this I've never carried bullets in my gun—just blanks.'

'Blanks? What are blanks?' asked Josiah.

'Dummy bullets,' said the Sheriff. 'They make a loud bang when you pull the trigger, but nothing comes out of the barrel. You see, in all my years as Sheriff of Deadwood I've never needed to use a gun with real bullets. Nobody ever does anything wrong here, so I've never had to shoot anybody.'

'Until now,' put in Martha.

'Until now,' agreed the Sheriff. A gloomy silence fell on the waiting-room group as they realised they were back to where they started. The Custard Kid had a gun, he had Calamity Kate as a hostage, and he was going to get away if they didn't think of something before the stage came in.

'There's only one thing for it,' said Barnaby, breaking the silence. The others looked at him hopefully. 'We'll have to get the Custard Kid's gun away from him.'

'Oh yes. I suppose you want me to just walk out there and say to him "Excuse me, Mr Custard, but would you mind giving me your gun? You see mine only has blanks, and I want to shoot you." '

Barnaby ignored the Sheriff's sarcasm and explained his plan. 'The Sheriff has a rope on his belt. We can lasso the gun!'

'But I'm no good with a lasso,' moaned the Sheriff.

'No, but I am,' Barnaby said calmly. 'I spend half my time, sitting on the hitching rail practising with an old rope. Why I can lasso a fly at twenty yards.'

'But as soon as you open that creaky old door the Custard Kid will draw his gun and shoot Calamity Kate,' objected Martha.

'I won't go through that door,' said Barnaby with a smile. 'Above this waiting-room there is another room. A door leads out from that room onto a balcony, and the balcony is directly above the Custard Kid's head. All I have to do is lower the rope from the balcony, hook Custard's gun from his holster and pull it up. He'll be harmless then!'

'That's brilliant boy,' gasped the Sheriff in admiration. 'Do you think it will work?'

'Of course,' said Barnaby confidently. 'And this way no one will get hurt.'

So the Sheriff gave the boy his rope and young Barnaby set off for the stairway to the upstairs room.

And in that dusty little stage-coach waiting-room twenty-seven spiders had listened breathlessly to Barnaby's plan. They busily set about making tiny lassos out of their sticky threads, and they spent the rest of that hot summer's afternoon trying to lasso the flies.

12

'Somebody's Taken My Gun'

Barnaby crept to the edge of the balcony and lowered the loop of the rope over the rail. Slowly it snaked down past the Custard Kid's right ear and stopped as Barnaby realised he was going to hit him on the shoulder if he went on. A fly buzzed along the street and chose that moment to settle on Custard Kid's nose. Custard lazily raised his right hand to brush away the fly. Barnaby jerked the rope up like lightning, and Custard's hand missed the rope by a whisker.

Sweat poured from Barnaby's forehead as he realised how close he had been to having his plan ruined by something as small as a fly. But Custard was dozing peacefully, so Barnaby edged the rope along a few inches to the right and lowered it again. This time his aim was perfect, and the noose dropped neatly over the handle of the gun. With a gentle tug the loop tightened, then a steady pull brought the gun out of its holster and on its way up to Barnaby.

'Whew,' whispered Barnaby, as he took the gun from the lasso and aimed it at the Custard Kid standing below. 'All right. You can come out now Sheriff,' he yelled.

The door of the waiting-room opened and out came the Sheriff pointing his gun at the Custard Kid. (The gun had no bullets in, of course, but Custard didn't know that.) The Custard Kid's hand flew to his holster for his gun—he raised his arm and aimed straight between the Sheriff's eyes. That was when he realised that he wasn't holding a gun. He looked at his empty hand. He looked at his empty holster. He forgot to put on his tough-talking voice, and said, rather sadly, 'Somebody's taken my gun.'

'That's right Custard,' Barnaby called down. 'Now just raise your hands above your head, and don't move.' The Custard Kid looked up at the balcony and saw his own gun pointing at him. He raised his hands.

'Well, Custard,' said the Sheriff proudly, 'this time I've got you.'

'You may have me, Sheriff,' agreed the Custard Kid, 'but you don't have the jewels. And what's more, I'm not going to tell you where I've hidden them.' Custard's great escape plan had gone wrong, and he was feeling very sulky.

The Quick Draw Contest

Sheriff Sam Simple ordered the Custard Kid back into the waiting-room, where he kept him covered, while Martha went out to release Calamity Kate, and Barnaby came downstairs to join them.

'If the Custard Kid won't tell you where the jewels are, then you ought to shoot him, Sheriff,' suggested Barnaby.

'Oh no, you can't do that!' cried Kate, coming in the door and rubbing her wrist which was sore from the handcuff.

'Why not?' asked the Sheriff, who was very puzzled to find Kate trying to protect the man who had kidnapped her.

Kate felt that she could hardly say, 'You can't shoot him because he's my hero,' so instead she explained, 'Well if you shoot him, he'll never be able to tell you where the jewels are hidden.'

'That's true,' admitted the Sheriff, who could see the sense in that.

'That's very true,' agreed the Custard Kid, who wasn't very keen on being shot.

'I've a better idea Sheriff. Why don't you have a duel with the Custard Kid?' suggested

Kate, who had always dreamed of having two men fighting over her. 'If the Custard Kid wins then he goes free, and he takes the jewels and me,' said Kate.

'And what about if I win?' asked the Sheriff, doubtfully.

'The Custard Kid must agree that if you kill him, he will tell you where the jewels are hidden,' answered Kate.

The Sheriff scratched his head because that didn't sound quite right. 'I'm sorry Miss Kate,' he said, 'but it wouldn't work. You see I don't have any bullets in my gun, only blanks.'

A broad grin spread across the face of the Custard Kid. 'That is marvellous Sheriff,' he cried. The others turned and looked at him in surprise. 'You see, Sheriff, I only have blanks in my gun too!'

The Sheriff's mouth fell wide open in surprise as he realised he'd been tricked.

'Sheriff! This is not good enough,' came a shrill voice from the corner of the room. It was Martha Hepgutt, and she was still angry at the weakness of the Sheriff. 'This man has got to be made to give up the jewels, and be brought to justice. And if you don't do your duty I'll report you to the next town council meeting and make sure you get the sack!'

'Martha doesn't often lose her temper, Sam,

but when she does, she means what she says,' added her husband, Josiah.

'I don't really see what I can do, if he won't tell where the jewels are,' grumbled the Sheriff.

'I'll tell you what we'll do, Sheriff,' the Custard Kid suggested. 'We'll have that gunfight, just the way Miss Kate suggested.'

'But we can't ...' the Sheriff began.

'No, listen,' Custard went on. 'We'll make it a quick draw contest. The first man to draw his gun and fire is the winner. If you win, I promise on my honour as a cowboy that I'll give myself up and stand trial.'

'And if the Custard Kid wins, then he goes free with the jewels,' piped up Barnaby.

'Agreed?' asked Custard.

'Agreed,' said the Sheriff, turning to Martha.

'Agreed,' said Martha.

'Agreed,' said Calamity Kate. And they went out into the street to prepare for the contest.

14

The Slowest Gun in the West

The customers in the Buffalo Ben Saloon were having a day they would remember all their lives. First a robbery, then a kidnapping, followed by a daring rescue, and now a gunfight, all happening under their noses.

The Custard Kid moved down to the south end of the street to practise—and he was good.

At the north end of the street the Sheriff was practising, and it was clear that a centipede could have tied its bootlaces faster than Sam Simple could draw his gun. First the Sheriff forgot which side his gun was on. When he found it, after a desperate search, he struggled to pull it out of the holster and succeeded in dropping it on his big toe. Martha Hepgutt was horrified. 'Sheriff Sam Simple,' she yelled, 'my grandmother could draw faster than you and she's 106 years old.'

For the Sheriff this was the last straw. He'd been nagged, threatened and insulted by Martha all afternoon, and he'd had enough. He turned to her and growled 'Let's see if you can do any better, Martha.'

Martha's face lit up with excitement as she jumped to her feet. 'Certainly, Sheriff. Just give me that gun and holster.'

Barnaby, Josiah and Kate sat on the steps of the stage-coach waiting-room and watched in disbelief as Martha buckled on the gun and began to practise. Their disbelief turned to pure amazement when they saw how fast the old lady was.

'Where did you learn to draw a gun so fast, Martha?' asked Kate.

'Oh, every weekend I play at gunfights with my grandchildren. I always wanted to be in a real gunfight though, and I suppose this is the nearest I'll ever get to it,' answered Martha with a sigh. 'Now then, Sheriff, bring on the Custard Kid. I'm going to teach him a lesson he'll never forget.'

15

The Fastest Gun in the West

The Custard Kid and Martha Hepgutt stood back to back, and made the oddest pair of gun-fighters you could ever wish to see. Custard was six foot two, and looked so skinny that you would wonder if he had the strength to hold a gun. Martha was just four foot six, and looked a perfectly sweet old lady except for two things: the gun on her hip, and the expression on her face, which looked like a tigress about to go into battle.

'I'm going to count to three,' said the Sheriff. 'You each take three paces forward, and on the count of three you turn and fire. Understand?'

The two gunfighters nodded grimly, and the Sheriff moved away to join Kate, Barnaby and Josiah on the steps of the stage-coach waiting-room. 'Ready?' called the Sheriff. The Custard Kid nodded his head and licked his lips nervously.

'I'm ready,' Martha called. The sun beat down on the gunfighters, and glinted on the steel rims of Martha's spectacles. But the glinting spectacles looked dull compared with the fiery sparks of adventure that lit up Martha's eyes.

'One,' the Sheriff called. The Custard Kid and Martha took a step.

'Two,' Custard's hand moved towards his gun. He slipped it halfway out of its holster and began to turn.

'Three.' As the Sheriff called the last number

Custard's gun was already in his hand, he had turned round and he had fired. Martha hadn't even reached for her gun. A stunned silence fell on the street as the echoes of Custard's shot faded into the distance. The first to break the silence was Barnaby.

'He cheated!'

'Cheat!' everyone in the saloon roared.

'I did not cheat,' Custard cried.

'Cheat, cheat, cheat,' they roared back.

'I fired on the count of three,' he protested.

'Yes, but you drew your gun on the count of two,' the Sheriff answered angrily.

'You good for nothing rattlesnake!' squawked the excited Martha, using language she wouldn't dream of using in church. 'You pointy-nosed drainpipe—you jug-eared jack-ass. How dare you cheat. You try that again and I'll fill you full of lead,' she threatened.

'But you only have blanks in your gun,' Custard objected.

'Very well, then. I'll fill you full of blanks,' answered Martha triumphantly.

'Now then, stop quarrelling you two, and let's get on with the contest. I suggest that, as Custard cheated, you draw again,' the Sheriff said.

'Oh very well,' Custard agreed sulkily. He felt very guilty, because he knew he had cheated and, even worse, everyone had seen him cheat.

46

16

The Two Gun-shots

Martha Hepgutt and the Custard Kid stood back to back once more. 'One,' shouted the Sheriff. They each took a step away from the other. 'Two.' Everyone held their breath and watched Custard's hand to see if he would draw the gun before the count of three. He didn't.

'Three.' The two gunfighters spun around exactly together, like two wheels on the same axle. Two hands went for two guns so fast that the spectators saw only a blur of movement such as you would see if you tried to watch the wing-beat of a fly.

'Bang-bang.' Two gun-shots rang out along Deadwood's silent street. Two gun-shots, one a fraction of a second before the other. But which one?

The Sheriff turned to Kate to see who she thought had fired that first shot. Kate shrugged her shoulders, bewildered. He turned to Barnaby and Barnaby shook his head, puzzled. Lastly he turned to Josiah. 'Don't ask me Sheriff,' said the old man.

The Custard Kid knew who had fired the first shot. He slid his gun back into his holster and walked towards Martha with his right hand out-stretched. 'Congratulations, Mrs Hepgutt. You beat me fair and square,' he announced for the whole town to hear. Martha took his hand and shook it. She looked warmly over the top of her spectacles at the Custard Kid and spoke gently so that only he could hear.

'Good boy,' she murmured. 'You won't regret it.' For old Martha Hepgutt knew who had won the contest. She knew that, even though she had drawn her gun faster than she ever had in her life, the first shot had not been fired by her. It had been fired by the Custard Kid.

'I hope this will stay a secret between you and me,' Custard whispered.

'You can trust me, son,' replied Martha with a wink. She turned to the Sheriff and called, 'He's all yours Mr Simple. Come and take him. But you make sure he gets a fair trial.'

Everyone crowded around Martha to con-gratulate her on her victory, but their celebra-tions were cut short by Barnaby, who looked up to see a cloud of dust rolling down the street. 'It's the Hollywood stage!' he cried, and so it was.

Everything in Deadwood stopped for the great event of the week—the arrival of the Holly-wood stage. Even the arrest of the Custard Kid

took second place in the interest of the Deadwood citizens as they crowded around to see
who the stage had brought in this time. In fact
the stage had only one passenger. The coach
door opened and out stepped a tubby little man
with a neat black suit, a black hat and a round,
smiling face.

He looked around at the waiting crowd and
announced, 'I'm the Chief Judge of this state.
My name's Judge Justin.'

The Sheriff stepped forward and welcomed
him. 'We're very pleased to see you, Judge Justin. You're just in time for a trial.'

The Courtroom at the Copper Nugget

Judge Justin was the chief judge of the state because he was the *best* judge in the state. Not only was he perfectly fair, but he was also very well organised, as he showed in Deadwood that afternoon. He decided to hold the trial of the Custard Kid in one of the saloons, as the old courthouse was in such bad repair. He appointed twelve of the Copper Nugget customers to be the jury and arranged evidence and witnesses to show both sides of Custard Kid's case. Within half an hour of his arrival, Judge Justin was ready to begin.

'Custard Kid,' he said from his seat behind the bar of the Copper Nugget, 'You are hereby charged with the kidnapping of Miss Calamity Kate. How do you plead—guilty or not guilty?'

The Jury Decides

The Custard Kid looked down at the floor miserably. 'Not guilty,' his voice croaked, though his face looked as if it was saying 'Guilty.'

The charge of kidnapping was very serious, and the case against the Custard Kid looked very strong, as witness after witness described how he had handcuffed Kate to the hitching rail, gagged her, and threatened her with a gun. The Judge called Barnaby as a witness, and it was then he discovered that it was the boy, and not the Sheriff, who was to be thanked for saving Kate.

'Sheriff,' said the Judge, 'has young Barnaby Tupper been rewarded for his bravery?'

'No, your honour,' answered Sam Simple.

'Well, he ought to be,' the Judge declared. 'We can't have good citizens like Barnaby risking their lives for nothing. I hereby order you to pay the boy 100 dollars reward for his part in the rescue of Calamity Kate.'

'Yes, your honour, anything you say sir,' said the Sheriff. He drew a large wallet from his pocket and counted five twenty-dollar bills into Barnaby's hand. Barnaby looked at the fortune that had come to him so unexpectedly, then dashed out of the saloon door and down the road.

'Hey ... I haven't finished questioning the boy,' called the Judge. 'Oh, never mind. Call the next witness—call Miss Calamity Kate.'

Kate stepped forward and took the oath to tell the truth. To everyone's surprise, she was the only one who spoke in defence of the Custard Kid. 'Judge-your-honour-high-sir,' she pleaded. 'I want you to know that the Custard Kid was a perfect gentleman when he kidnapped me. He didn't hurt me one little bit.'

'But he handcuffed you to the railings!' objected the judge.

'Only because he wanted to make sure that I went to Hollywood with him. He obviously fell in love with me at first sight, and couldn't bear the thought of losing me,' explained Kate dreamily.

'Uh?' exclaimed Custard, for that was the first he knew about it.

'But he stuffed your mouth full of ribbons,' the judge reminded her.

'Of course he did,' Kate answered. 'It was terribly dusty in that street and he put the ribbons in my mouth to keep the dust out.'

'But he threatened to shoot you,' said the judge desperately.

'I know, but he couldn't have meant it, because he didn't have any bullets in his gun,' replied Kate.

'Oh, I give up,' said the Judge. 'I leave it up to the jury to decide. Miss Kate may not have minded being kidnapped, but if you think she was then you must find the Custard Kid guilty,' he instructed the jury.

And after a long, fierce argument, that's just what the jury did.

19

The Sentence

'Custard Kid, you have been found guilty of the crime of kidnapping,' said the Judge, sternly. 'For this crime I could sentence you to thirty years imprisonment,' he added. A gasp of horror ran through the court. 'Have you anything to say to the court before I pass sentence?' asked the judge.

After a long, uncomfortable silence Custard straightened his shoulders, raised his chin and looked the judge in the eye. With a slight tremble in his voice he began his plea.

'Your honour, I've done wrong, and I know it. But I want to explain that I didn't do it because I'm a bad man at heart, but because I was a foolish man.' The judge nodded wisely, and allowed him to go on. Custard turned to the jury, and spoke half to them and half to himself. 'When I was a little boy, just knee high to a grasshopper, my daddy died, and my mom had to struggle to look after us. I was the youngest in the family and I had ten older sisters—most of my clothes were handed down from them, and I can tell you I looked pretty stupid going to school in girls' clothes. And when I grew up

it wasn't much better, because I was so tall and skinny and the other cowboys on the ranch used to bully me and call me Custard. So I had to learn to talk tough and act tough and handle a gun even though it went against my nature. And then I had the chance of a job as a stunt-man in Hollywood and I thought it was the best chance I'd ever had in my life to make a new start; to make a lot of money to send home to mom and let her live in comfort as she deserves. All I had to do was get on the Hollywood stage. When I came into Deadwood today to wait for the stage it seemed as if all my dreams were coming true. Then when I got into that silly muddle over the bag of jewels, and I saw the Sheriff coming at me with his handcuffs, I panicked. I saw myself going to jail for a crime I hadn't committed—I saw myself missing the stage, and I saw my dreams flying out of the window. Yes, I just panicked. I grabbed that poor, innocent Miss Kate and tried to make my getaway. That was a stupid thing to do, and now I know it. But, your honour, I swear to you I never meant to hurt her, and if you show me mercy I'll never do a wrong thing in my life again.' The Custard Kid finished and looked around the court. The silence was like a graveyard at midnight, broken only by a gentle 'plop' as a huge tear from Calamity Kate hit the floor.

The judge blew his nose loudly to clear the tears from his own eyes, and tried to sound stern as he spoke to the Custard Kid. 'As you say, young man, you have been very foolish, but I don't believe that you are bad at heart. It would be sad to see you go to jail. On the other hand, you have been found guilty by the jury and I must pass sentence. I therefore give you two years of probation for this offence.'

'*Probation*. What's that?' asked Custard.

'It means you are free to go ....' explained the Sheriff.

'Oh, good,' cried Custard in relief.

'But,' went on the Judge, 'you must stay out of trouble ...'

'Of course,' Custard said eagerly.

'And you must report to Sheriff Simple once a week,' the Judge ended.

Custard's face fell. 'But how can I report to the Sheriff if I'm going to Hollywood? It's a thousand miles away!'

'That's true,' answered the Judge, scratching his head. 'Let me see. If you could find a respectable citizen in Hollywood who would promise to look after you and make sure you stay out of trouble then I might just let you go; otherwise you'll have to stay in Deadwood for the next two years.'

'Judge-your-honour-high-sir,' cried Kate, jumping to her feet and waving her hand to attract the judge's attention.

'Yes, Miss Kate?' he asked.

'I was just thinking that *I'm* going to Hollywood on the stage, and *I'm* a respectable citizen.' She blushed, shyly as she suggested, 'How about letting me look after him?'

'But Miss Kate, this is the man who tried to kidnap you!' objected Sheriff Sam Simple.

'Oh but Sheriff, you wouldn't want to see me go to Hollywood alone and unprotected would you? Don't you see, the Custard Kid could look after me while I looked after him,' she argued.

'Well ...' said Sheriff Sam Simple, doubtfully.

'I have no objections,' said the Judge. 'How about you Sheriff?'

'Oh very well,' agreed the Sheriff grumpily.

'That's settled then. The Custard Kid is free to leave in Miss Kate's custody, or should I say Custard-y?' the judge joked. 'Court is dismissed.'

A huge cheer broke out in the courtroom, hats were flung in the air, Martha thumped out a happy tune on the piano, and, as the courtroom was also a bar, drinks were bought to celebrate the fact that Justice had been done.

The Hollywood Stage

The celebrations in the Copper Nugget were cut short by the driver of the stage-coach. He looked over the top of the swing doors into the saloon and yelled. 'Hey there, Judge Justin, I've held the stage for you for three hours. I'll have to leave soon if we're going to be in Hollywood on time.'

'I'm coming,' the judge replied.

'So are we!' called Calamity Kate, clinging tightly to the Custard Kid's arm, and leading him outside.

The saloon quickly emptied as everyone followed the travellers out to the waiting stage-coach to say goodbye and good-luck. The judge climbed on board the stage-coach and was followed by Kate who stopped on the top step and look around.

'Where's young Barnaby?' she asked. 'I wanted to thank him for rescuing me.'

'I'm here, Miss Kate,' called Barnaby as he ran down the street from the old courthouse with a cat clutched in one arm, and a battered old suitcase in the other. He pushed his way through the crowd to the door of the stage-coach where Custard was saying a special goodbye to Martha Hepgutt. The citizens of Deadwood could hardly recognise Barnaby, for his sun-bleached hair was actually brushed neatly into place, and instead of his faded dungarees he was wearing a black suit and clean white shirt. He looked as smart as Judge Justin himself.

'Oh, it's nice to see you before I go, Barnaby,' said Kate. 'I wanted to say goodbye and . . .'

'But I'm coming too,' interrupted Barnaby.

'You're what?'

'All my life I've wanted to go to Hollywood, to look after all the horses they use in their films. I've never been able to save enough money for the stage-coach fare, but the Sheriff's hundred dollar reward has changed that,' explained Barnaby.

'Climb aboard then partner,' cried Kate happily.

Barnaby first turned to Martha Hepgutt and shyly asked her if she would mind looking after his cat while he was away. 'I'd be proud to,' Martha answered, and she reached forward and kissed him on the cheek. 'Good luck son.'

He passed his suitcase up to the driver, and the driver placed it on the roof of the stage-coach next to two bags. They were two green travelling bags with the initials 'C.K.' on the side.

The last to climb aboard was the Custard Kid. He turned to the waiting crowd and said, 'Well cheerio folks. I want to thank you for giving me this second chance—I won't let you down.'

At last everyone was on board, the driver cracked his whip and the Hollywood stage moved out. Calamity Kate, the Custard Kid and Barnaby Tupper leaned out of the stage-coach windows and waved to the people of Deadwood. The townsfolk waved back and cheered, while in the waiting-room twenty-seven spiders crowded to the window where twenty-seven legs were waved in farewell.

'We'll be seeing you Kate,' called Josiah Hepgutt, 'in the movies!'

Kate grinned back happily and began to sing her audition song as the stage moved out of sight.

'I can sing and I can dance,
I can act and play guitar.
If I'm given half a chance,
I will be a great big star.'

'Hmm,' Martha Hepgutt muttered to herself. 'Probably just as well they're *silent* movies!'

And the Custard Kid and Calamity Kate drove off into the sunset.

The End